SURELY
SURELY
MARISOL
RAINEY

ERIN ENTRADA KELLY

SURELY SURELY

MARISOL RAINEY

 GREENWILLOW BOOKS
An Imprint of HarperCollinsPublishers

Surely Surely Marisol Rainey

The text of this book is set in Garth Graphic. Book design by Sylvie Le Floc'h.

Library of Congress Cataloging-in-Publication Data

Names: Kelly, Erin Entrada, author.
Title: Surely surely Marisol Rainey / by Erin Entrada Kelly.
Description: First edition. | New York : Greenwillow Books, an imprint of HarperCollins Publishers, [2022] | Audience: Ages 8-12. | Audience: Grades 4-6. | Summary: "One of Marisol's least-favorite things is gym class—especially when Coach Decker announces that they will be playing kickball—so Marisol and her best friend Jada ask the best (and stinkiest) athlete they know—Marisol's big brother Oz—for help"—Provided by publisher.
Identifiers: LCCN 2022000015 | ISBN 9780062970459 (hardback) | ISBN 9780062970473 (ebook)
Subjects: CYAC: Kickball—Fiction. | Self-confidence—Fiction. | Best friends—Fiction. | Friendship—Fiction. | LCGFT: Novels.
Classification: LCC PZ7.1.K45 Su 2022 | DDC [Fic]—dc23
LC record available at https://lccn.loc.gov/2022000015

22 23 24 25 26 PC/LSCH 10 9 8 7 6 5 4 3 2 1
First Edition

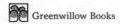 Greenwillow Books

To Danny

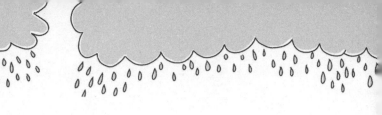

CONTENTS

NICE TRY, MARISOL

Marisol Rainey keeps a list in her head. She calls it her List of Favorites.

Ice Cream: Vanilla

Movie: A Dog's Life

Animal: cats

Food: Lumpia

Snack: Jelly beans

Friend: Jada

Teacher: Ms. Ruby

Day of the week: Saturday

Color: green

Her best friend, Jada George, has a list, too. Marisol and Jada like to compare their lists because it's interesting to see all the ways they are the same and all the ways they are different. For example: Marisol's favorite ice cream flavor is vanilla, because vanilla goes with everything. You can use vanilla for banana splits, which is one of Marisol's favorite foods. You can pour chocolate syrup on top of vanilla. You can mix peanuts or sprinkles with vanilla. You can put vanilla on top of apple pies, brownies, and peach cobbler. And it always tastes delicious.

Jada disagrees. She says vanilla is *bo-ring*. She likes mint chocolate chip, because it has tiny pieces of chocolate in it.

Marisol's older brother, Osgood—everyone calls him "Oz"—says it's too hard to pick favorites when there are so many things to like. But Jada and Marisol don't think so. To them, their Lists of Favorites make perfect sense.

Marisol and Jada also have lists of their least favorites.

Lemon is Marisol's least-favorite ice cream flavor. For Jada, it's butter pecan.

Mustard is Marisol's least-favorite condiment. For Jada, it's mayonnaise.

Radishes are Marisol's least-favorite food. For Jada, it's grapefruit.

Jada's and Marisol's Least-Favorite Foods

Marisol and Jada spend a lot of time discussing the things they like and don't like. Jada is a philosopher, so she thinks about stuff that no one else considers, which means she likes to ask questions, such as "Would you rather . . . ?"

Would you rather eat radishes or drink mayonnaise for the rest of your life? Would you rather eat only nachos forever or never eat them again? Would you rather give up banana splits or jelly beans?

Jada also asks things like *Would you rather clean Beans's litter box every day or clean your room?* Because she knows those are two of Marisol's least-favorite things to do.

Beans is Marisol's orange cat.

MARISOL'S
Least-Favorite Things

#5. Waking up early in the morning.
#4. Helping mom find lost stuff.
#3. Cleaning Beans's Litter Box.
#2. Cleaning Room.

Jada's
Least-Favorite Things

#5. Going to the dentist.
#4. Grocery shopping with mom.
#3. Helping Dad with dishes.
#2. Going to bed.

Even though Jada and Marisol don't have identical lists, they both agree that their number-one Least-Favorite Thing to Do is:

GYM CLASS!

Gym class at Getty Elementary School isn't always terrible. Sometimes Marisol has fun, like when they play hopscotch. And she likes Coach Decker. She doesn't like him as much as Ms. Ruby—Ms. Ruby is number one on her Favorite Teachers list—but he's nice, even though his face shrivels like a raisin when he's concentrating on his stopwatch, and his whistle is loud and shrill. Coach Decker shouts a lot, but not in a mean way. When Sherry Roat runs the bases, Coach Decker shouts, "Go, Sherry, go!" When Evie Smythe scores points in basketball, he shouts, "All right! Go, Evie!" And when Danny Grant wins the shuttle runs, he says, "Way to go, Danny!"

Marisol likes when Coach Decker cheers for her, even though she never runs the bases or scores points or wins races. But once—just once—she would like to hear him shout, "Way to go, Marisol!" just like he does for Sherry and Evie and Danny.

ANY OTHER THURSDAY

Marisol's Terrible Thursday starts like any other Thursday. She suffers through math. She listens during social studies. She does worksheets in science. Then it's time for recess. At recess, she plays Food Tag, which is one of her favorite games. It's like Freeze Tag, except you yell out the name of a food before you unfreeze someone, and it can't be a food that's already been said.

Marisol loves playing Food Tag because she knows a lot of foods that her classmates don't.

That's because her mother is from the Philippines, which means Marisol eats Filipino food that no one else has ever heard of, like lumpia, pancit, and chicken adobo. She loves lumpia so much that one of her five stuffed animal cats is named Lumpia. The others are Banana Split, Pot Roast, Hi-C, and Nacho.

At first, it's a normal Thursday. Life is good. After Marisol wins Food Tag, she and Jada walk to gym class. It's free play day, which means they can do any activity they want. Jada and Marisol always choose hula-hooping because they like to compete with each other. Some days, Marisol hula-hoops the longest. Other days, it's Jada. Today, Marisol wins by seven seconds. At the end of class, they are both exhausted. Hula-hooping is harder than it looks.

Then Coach Decker gathers them all together and says the worst five words Marisol has heard all day.

Surely the worst five words she's heard all *week*, maybe all *year*, possibly her *entire life*.

Evie Smythe cheers. "Oh, I *love* kickball!" she says, adjusting her fox ears. Evie Smythe loves wearing fox ears to school. They look a lot like Marisol's cat ears, but Evie insists they are *fox* ears, *not* cat ears. Marisol doesn't wear her cat ears to school, but if she did, she would let everyone know that they were *cat* ears, not *fox* ears.

Evie Smythe

"Good, because we'll spend two weeks on it," Coach Decker says.

Marisol's belly plummets to her sneakers. She locks eyes with Jada, whose expression looks just like hers: not-smiling and almost-frowning. Two whole weeks!

Coach Decker tells them to tidy up the gym equipment, and Evie talks about kickball the whole time.

"I can kick the ball *so far!*" Evie tells Danny Grant as she carries a paddleball set to its plastic bin. "Practically from one side of the field to the other."

Marisol thinks that Evie talks to Danny because he's the shyest kid in class, which means he barely says anything, which means Evie gets to talk as much as she wants.

"I'm *the best* at kickball," Evie continues.

It isn't very nice for Evie to be so braggy, in

Marisol's opinion. Then again, Marisol's also a little jealous. Evie is good at all sports. It isn't fair.

When it's time to get in a single-file line, Marisol acts like she doesn't have a care in the world, but her heart goes *thump-thump-thump*. She barely even reacts when Jada taps her shoulder.

"Felix says he can talk to animals," Jada whispers.

Marisol doesn't turn around. They aren't supposed to talk in line. Besides, all she can think is *KICKBALL, KICKBALL, KICKBALL,* like a bright, blinking sign.

Marisol has never played kickball before, but she already knows she won't be good at it. Sure, she can play hopscotch and tag, and she can hula-hoop for a long time. She doesn't even mind taking part in a race sometimes at recess, especially if it's a skipping race. But kickball is a *team* sport. Everyone counts on you. If you mess up, you mess *everything* up. The spotlight shines on you when you kick. The spotlight shines on you when you pitch. The spotlight shines on you when you catch. The spotlight shines on you when you run the bases.

Surely Marisol will burst into flames under all those spotlights.

"Earth to Marisol, Earth to Marisol," Jada whispers behind her.

"Kickball" is all Marisol can say.

She does not say it in a joyful voice.

She does not say it in a cheerful voice.

Think of the way you'd greet your worst enemy.

That's how she says "kickball."

Jada understands right away.

"I know," she whispers. "Furchtbar."

Furchtbar is a German word. Jada and Marisol taught themselves all kinds of words in other languages so they can speak in code whenever they want.

Furchtbar means "terrible."

THE BRAIN TRAIN

Marisol is still thinking about kickball on Friday night when Dadhead calls.

Dadhead is the Rainey family nickname for Marisol's father. He works as an electrician on an oil rig in the Gulf of Mexico. He takes a helicopter from Getty, Louisiana, all the way to the rig. He's home only one week out of each month, but he calls every Monday, Wednesday, and Friday night at 7:00 p.m. When Mrs. Rainey's laptop chimes from the dining room table, Oz cries out,

"Dadhead! Dadhead!" and they all gather around to talk to him.

DaDHeaD

Only Mr. Rainey's head and shoulders appear on the screen. He's usually wearing his blue work coveralls. There is a sink behind him because he sets up his laptop in the rig's mess hall, which is what they call the dining room.

"Hello, hello!" he says. "How was everyone's day?"

Oz tells Dadhead about his soccer practice and video games, and Mrs. Rainey tells him about her day at Getty Middle School, where she's a science teacher. Then Dadhead looks at Marisol. She's wearing her cat ears and holding Nacho tight because it makes her feel better.

"Why're you so quiet, Scraps?" Dadhead asks.

Marisol likes when her dad calls her "Scraps." It's from a Charlie Chaplin movie called *A Dog's Life*. They watched it together once. Dadhead kept falling asleep, but it didn't matter. He was there.

Marisol shrugs.

"Anything on your mind?" Dadhead asks.

Marisol's mind is full of many things. She has one thought, then another, then another, like a long train going down the tracks. A Brain Train.

But she doesn't want to say any of her thoughts out loud. Not right now, anyway. What if Oz makes fun of her? What if Dadhead says, "That's nothing to worry about, Scraps"? What if Mom tells her, "Don't worry, anak. Everything will be fine"? That's what usually happens when Marisol shares her worries. She knows her family loves her and wants to make her feel better, but sometimes it feels like they don't take her seriously.

So Marisol changes the subject.

"Felix Powell says he can talk to animals," she tells her father.

Oz rolls his eyes. "That is so dumb."

Oz is twelve. He thinks a lot of things are dumb.

"You've got to be kitten me," Dadhead says.

Dadhead loves puns.

Mrs. Rainey laughs and rolls her eyes. "Can Felix tell Beans to stop tearing up my couch?" she asks.

Beans constantly scratches the sofa cushions. That's what he's doing now, in fact. The couch is named Betty Bigmouth, because it likes to eat things like Mrs. Rainey's phone and all the remote controls. No one knows the couch's name except Marisol and Jada. Marisol is the one who named her, because she believes all important things should have their own names.

Beans has a scratching post, but he prefers Betty. According to Mrs. Rainey, cats scratch things to mark objects with their scent, to sharpen their claws, or just for a good stretch. No one knows why Beans likes Betty more than the scratching post, though.

"Tell Felix to watch out for oysters," Dadhead says. "They're very shellfish."

Oz and Mrs. Rainey groan, but they're smiling.

"Good one, Will," Mrs. Rainey says.

Marisol hugs Nacho tighter. Usually she laughs at her dad's jokes, but she doesn't feel like laughing right now, because the Brain Train is still chugging.

Chug, chug, chug.

IN A DEMOCRACY

Marisol is excited about recess on Monday because she didn't get to see Jada all weekend. Jada was at Mr. George's house, which is way across town. Marisol is happy that Jada gets to spend time with her dad, but she likes it better when Jada is at her mom's, because Ms. George lives only three blocks away from the Raineys.

"Did you have fun at your dad's?" Marisol asks as they dart out to the playground. It's hot,

hot, hot outside, but nobody cares. Everyone is just happy to be free.

"Yeah, but I left Cornelius there," Jada says. She frowns. "Now I have to wait two whole weeks to see him again."

Cornelius is Jada's favorite stuffed animal. He's a black-and-white dog with floppy ears that Marisol once rescued from the claw machine at Dazzo's, her favorite restaurant. Marisol rescued it on the first try, so it only took one quarter.

CORNELIUS GOLIGHTLY, stuffed animal

CORNELIUS
goLigHTLy,
PhD.
←

The dog's full name is Cornelius Golightly. Jada named him after a civil rights activist and "public intellectual." Marisol doesn't know what a "public intellectual" is, but it sounds smart, so she assumes that it is.

Jada and Marisol make their way toward the Big Tree, where the kids in their grade always meet to play Food Tag or Red Light, Green Light. A bunch of kids are already there, standing in a little cluster. Evie Smythe is in the center with her arms crossed.

"It'll be good practice," Evie is saying. There's a basketball at her feet.

Marisol doesn't like the look of this. She leans closer to Jada and whispers, "What's going on?"

Jada shrugs. Felix and Danny are there, along with Isabella Sanchez and Lucas Richardson. It's the usual Food Tag crowd.

When Marisol and Jada walk up, Evie lifts her chin and says, "We're going to practice kickball at recess today," like it's all decided.

On the playground around them, kids swing on monkey bars, sail down slides, and climb the jungle gym. But it's quiet around the big oak tree. They're all staring at the ball sitting in front of Evie's bright purple sneakers.

"That's not a kickball," Jada finally says. "It's a basketball."

Evie sighs loudly. "I know, *dummy*. But we don't have a kickball."

Marisol narrows her eyes at Evie. "Jada isn't a dummy," she says, but she says it too quietly, because Evie doesn't hear. Instead, Evie snatches up the basketball and holds it in front of them.

"Trust me," Evie says. "This will be good practice. Basketballs are way heavier than kickballs. If you can kick a basketball, then just imagine how far the kickball will go! Kickballs are practically nothing."

Practically nothing? Marisol has never actually kicked a kickball, but she doesn't think they're practically nothing. They may not be as heavy and tough as basketballs, but there's plenty that could go wrong with a kickball.

FACE pLAnt →

mIssED cAtcH →

"I think it's a really bad idea to try to kick a basketball," Felix says. "We might break our toes."

Isabella Sanchez puts her hands on her hips. "*I* think Evie has a point. If we practice with this basketball, it'll just make us better kickball players."

"*Kickballers,*" Evie corrects.

Marisol notices a small squirrel sitting on the ground near Felix. Usually, squirrels scamper away when the kids gather at the Big Tree, but this one is sitting nice and still, as if it's considering whether or not to chime in.

Felix notices Marisol looking at the squirrel and says, "Oh, this is Reginald."

Jada raises her eyebrows. "Reginald?"

Felix shrugs. "That's what he says."

Evie rolls her eyes and sighs loudly again. She's very good at sighing.

She holds the basketball like a trophy. "Are we going to play kick basketball or what?" She glances toward Marisol and adds, "Food Tag is *so* babyish."

Marisol is the one who invented Food Tag, and everyone knows it. Evie Smythe is an expert at throwing invisible darts at Marisol's feelings. The first thing Evie ever said to Marisol was "What kind of name is *Marisol*, anyway?" That was last year, and Evie hasn't changed much since.

"In a democracy, people have a chance to vote," Jada says. She takes a step forward so she's standing right next to Evie. "That's what they did in ancient Greece. And last time I checked, we live in a *democracy*."

The word "democracy" first appeared in ancient Greece. It means "Rule by the people."

Marisol isn't sure what "democracy" means exactly, and by the looks of Felix, Isabella, Danny, and Lucas, they don't either. But if Jada says they should take a vote, they believe her.

"Would you rather play kick-basketball, which isn't even a real thing, or would you rather play an awesome game of Food Tag?" Jada says. "Raise your right hand for kick-basketball. Raise your left hand for an awesome game of Food Tag."

Evie tucks the basketball under her left arm and raises her right hand quicker than lightning. Isabella raises her right hand, too. But it's not to be, because everyone else raises their left hands—especially Felix. He even waves his hand back and forth and jumps up and down to really get his point across. Felix loves Food Tag almost as much as Marisol does. All of Felix's sudden movements startle Reginald, who scurries up the tree behind him.

"Food Tag wins!" Jada says.

Everyone cheers except Evie and Isabella. Marisol and Felix cheer the loudest.

"I'll be It!" Felix says. He usually volunteers to be It because he's anxious to start the game. Before they get started, though, Marisol taps his shoulder.

When Felix turns around, Marisol asks, "Why do you call the squirrel Reginald?"

Felix shrugs. "That's his name."

"Oh," Marisol says.

When the game begins, Marisol takes off with the others.

THE THING ABOUT
BEST FRIENDS

After school, Mrs. Rainey makes microwave popcorn for Jada and Marisol and they eat it out of an enormous bowl until their fingertips are covered with salt. (Marisol adds extra salt when Mrs. Rainey isn't looking.) Then they drink two big glasses of cold, cold water and go into the backyard. Marisol watches Jada climb to the knobbiest branch of the magnolia tree. Jada leans against the trunk and dangles one leg down. Marisol climbs to the branch just below Jada. She dangles her leg, too.

The tree is named Peppina.

"If you could talk to Beans, what would you say to him?" Jada asks.

Like any great philosopher, Jada comes up with a lot of hypothetical questions.

"Hypothetical" means an "imagined idea" or "a fictional example"

Marisol loves Beans so much that she named him after one of her favorite snacks: Jelly Beans. Marisol takes care of Beans all by herself, even though Mrs. Rainey didn't think she would. Beans likes to spend time with Marisol most of all. He even sleeps on her bed.

Marisol has had many conversations with Beans, but he's not the best listener. He usually falls asleep while she's talking, starts licking his paws, or just says *meow*. She doesn't mind, though. He's a cat, after all.

She never considered what she might ask him if he could talk back.

Marisol leans her head against Peppina's trunk. She's sweating, even though she's in the shade, because Louisiana humidity is so brutal.

"I would ask him if he's happy," she says.

Jada considers this, then nods. "Good answer," she says. "If he says no, you can ask why and then you can fix it."

Marisol thinks about other animals that she knows, including Daggers, the mean and scary German shepherd who lives nearby. She doesn't know his real name, but she thinks of him as "Daggers" because his teeth are pointy and sharp. At least she thinks they are. She's never actually seen them.

"What would you say to Daggers if you could talk to him?" Marisol asks.

Jada is afraid of Daggers, too.

"Please don't eat us," Jada says matter-of-factly.

"Good answer," Marisol says. She pulls off a little chip of bark and throws it to the ground for no reason. "Have you ever played kickball?"

"No, and I don't want to start," says Jada. "My dad says it isn't that hard, though."

That doesn't make Marisol feel much better. There are a lot of things that people say aren't that hard, but they're hard for Marisol. Mrs. Rainey told Marisol that swimming lessons would be fun, but Marisol didn't think so. Oz told her that riding a bike with one hand was easy, but it took a long time for Marisol to do it. Her class had learned to play T-ball in first grade and Dadhead said it would be "no problem," but it took twelve swings before Marisol even hit the ball. No one else took that many tries. Just Marisol.

Sometimes, what's easy for one person isn't easy for another.

Marisol knows that for sure.

"I told my dad to take care of Cornelius while I'm gone," says Jada. "Do you think he's really taking care of him, or is he just *saying* he's taking care of him?"

"I bet he's really taking care of him," Marisol replies, and she means it. Marisol has only met Jada's dad a few times, but he seems very nice, even though he says he won't drive Cornelius home because Jada needs to learn to stop forgetting things at his house. "They're probably doing all kinds of fun stuff," Marisol tells Jada. "Cornelius is on vacation."

CORNELIUS ON vacation with MR. GEORGE

"Thanks, Marisol," Jada says.

They sit in silence, feeling the heat on their skin.

Jada swings and swings her leg. Then she lets out a big sigh and says, "I'm worried about kickball, too."

That's the thing about best friends.

They always know what to say to each other.

QUEEN
OF KICKBALL

Neither Jada nor Marisol expects anything good to happen when they walk into gym class the next day. They assume Coach Decker will blow his whistle and march them to the field and force them to play kickball. Instead, Coach Decker is standing in the middle of the basketball court, holding a bucket of Popsicle sticks with a net bag full of kickballs at his feet.

The Popsicle sticks are not as exciting as they sound—there aren't any actual Popsicles—and everyone knows what the bucket means.

It means they are going to be separated into pairs.

"Let's pair up," Coach Decker says. He shakes the bucket. "Come get your sticks. Whoever you're paired with will be your partner for the rest of the week."

They all rush to the bucket, including Marisol. When she reaches her hand inside and wraps her fingers around a stick, she thinks: *Please pair me with Jada, please pair me with Jada, please pair me with Jada.* But there are twenty kids in the class, so she knows the chances that she'll get paired with Jada aren't very good.

The chance that I will be paired with Marisol is only five percent, mathematically speaking.

Marisol and Jada hurry toward each other as soon as they have their Popsicle sticks to see if they're a match. Jada's stick says UP. Marisol's says PEANUT BUTTER.

That is definitely not a match.

"Ay, naku," says Marisol. *Ay, naku* is a common Filipino expression to convey disappointment.

She wishes she could trade Popsicle sticks with the person who has DOWN, but it's against the rules.

Kids scurry around, looking for a match. Marisol does, too. Except she doesn't scurry toward Evie Smythe, because she surely *does not* want to be paired with Evie.

Danny's stick says COLD. He pairs with Lucas Richardson, who has HOT.

Jada finds Sherry Roat, who has DOWN.

Isabella Sanchez matches with Evie because she has BEAR and Evie has TEDDY.

Finally, Marisol finds Felix.

Marisol is disappointed that she isn't with Jada, but Felix is a good compromise because he's nice and he loves animals and maybe he can even talk to them, though Marisol isn't sure she believes it.

Most of all, Marisol is happy she isn't paired with Evie.

Coach Decker rolls a kickball toward each pair and says they'll be doing drills to prepare for their real-life kickball game. He tells them to stand across from one another, about seven feet apart. He puts bright orange cones on the floor to mark their spots.

"One of you will be the pitcher, so you have to roll the ball to your partner. And your partner will be the kicker, so they'll kick it— *gently*." Coach Decker holds up his index finger when he says the word "gently" to really get his point across. Some of the kids have already started rolling their balls before he even finishes explaining. But Marisol and Felix wait until he's done.

"You can start after I blow the whistle," Coach Decker continues. He throws a stern look toward the kids who have already started, including Evie and Isabella. "When I blow the whistle again, switch positions. The pitcher becomes the kicker. Got it?"

Felix smiles at Marisol. He's holding the kickball under his arm.

"Do you want to be the pitcher or the kicker first?" he asks.

Marisol wants to be neither, but she answers right away. "Pitcher!"

She thinks pitching will be easier than kicking.

Felix gives her the ball just as Coach Decker blows his whistle. The gym immediately explodes into activity. Kickballs fly everywhere, even though Coach Decker told them to kick gently. Kids have to chase the balls, and they're laughing and making noise as they're doing so, all while Coach Decker stands to the side, yelling, "Gently! Gently!" and "Focus!" and "Look where you want the ball to go!"

Felix doesn't kick the ball too hard, and Marisol is thankful for that. He kicks it right to her, so she doesn't even have to chase it.

"Do you think animals play games?" Felix asks as he waits for her to return the ball. "I mean, not like kickball. But their own games." He pauses. "Maybe I'll ask Reginald."

The animals play their own game: Pin the Snail on the Donkey

Marisol is only half listening. She's trying not to notice how hard Evie kicks the ball.

Evie even takes a few steps back before she kicks.

"This is called a *running start*," says Evie matter-of-factly.

Marisol can hear her because Evie isn't very far away. Evie is never far enough away, in Marisol's opinion.

"To build momentum, you have to get a running

start," continues Evie, as if she's the gym teacher.

Isabella has to chase the ball every time Evie kicks it. She doesn't look too thrilled.

Marisol and Felix have a good rhythm going. Pitch. Kick. Pitch. Kick. Marisol isn't even worried when Coach Decker blows the whistle again, because Felix made kicking look so easy. Felix didn't do any *running starts* like Evie, but he still kicked the ball. When Felix rolls the ball to Marisol, she kicks it, too . . . but the ball just skids a few feet and sputters to a stop.

"Ohmy*gosh!*" says Evie. She's holding her kickball in both hands. Isabella is waiting to kick, but Evie is too busy laughing. "My *grandma* kicks better than Marisol!"

Some kids laugh, but most of them are busy doing their own thing.

Marisol's heart races. Her cheeks warm. She looks for Jada, but she's on the other side of the gym.

"Don't listen to her," says Felix. Then he raises his voice a little higher. "She thinks she's the queen of kickball or something."

Evie Smythe, Queen of Kickball

Evie absently pitches the ball to Isabella but keeps her eyes on Felix. She puts her hand on her hip.

"I do NOT! I'm just really good at kickball!" Evie says. When the ball rolls back to her, she leans forward and snatches it up. "It's not my fault your *girlfriend* is so terrible at it!"

"She's not my girlfriend!" Felix says. He rolls his eyes and looks at Marisol. "Just ignore her."

Marisol smiles, even though she doesn't want to.

Evie always ruins everything.

EXTRAORDINARY SOMETHING

Surely the only thing worse than being terrible at sports is having an older brother or sister who is a fantastic athlete. When you have a sibling, there's always someone to compare yourself to.

Marisol is better than Oz at some things—like not being annoying and not making a mess in the kitchen—but sometimes Marisol wishes she was more like Oz. Especially right now, when she is sitting with her mom at Oz's soccer practice.

Oz plays for a team called the Tornadoes. They practice twice a week after school at a place called Sideco Park. Marisol and Mrs. Rainey bring foldout chairs and watch from the sidelines. Usually, Mrs. Rainey reads a book and Marisol sits and watches the team with one of her stuffed animals on her lap. She brings a different one every time so they all get a chance to have an outing. Today, she has Pot Roast.

Even though Marisol doesn't play soccer and doesn't really understand all the rules, she likes to cheer for Oz at the practices, and she likes to cheer for the Tornadoes during the games. She doesn't cheer too loudly, though. She just claps or says, "Way to go, Oz!" and sometimes her stuffed animals—like Pot Roast—clap, too.

Pot Roast cheers for Oz

There are only two things Marisol doesn't like about going to Oz's soccer practices. One, it's hot. Very hot.

Second is how Oz smells afterward. Charlie—that's the name of Mrs. Rainey's car—smells like dirty, sweaty socks the whole ride home. If Marisol ever made a list of Least-Favorite Smells, Oz would be on it after every soccer practice.

For now, though, Marisol is just grumpy about the heat.

"It's hot," she says. "Can we go to Armijo's after practice?"

Armijo's is an ice cream shop across from Sideco Park that has the most delicious banana splits in the world. Sometimes—not *all* the time, but *sometimes*—Mrs. Rainey takes them there. Armijo's is the best ice cream shop ever because it's a two-favorite-food place. Not only do they have banana splits, they also sell jelly beans.

"We'll see," Mrs. Rainey says without looking up from her mystery novel. Mrs. Rainey loves mysteries. The name of the book is *Arsenic and Adobo*, by Mia P. Manansala.

"Do you know who the bad guy is yet?" Marisol asks.

"Not yet," Mrs. Rainey says.

Mrs. Rainey is the smartest person Marisol

knows, but she isn't very good at solving mysteries. She usually never sees it coming, or she guesses wrong. Luckily, she doesn't work as a detective in real life.

On the field, Oz's coach, whose name is Coach Calandra, blows the whistle, and the Tornadoes scramble for a scrimmage. Marisol watches the players kick the ball from person to person, like it's no big deal at all. Oz even scores a goal and everyone cheers, including Marisol and Pot Roast. But the excitement doesn't last long because it's *so hot* outside.

"It's hot," Marisol says again.

Mrs. Rainey sighs. "Why don't you and Pot Roast go sit at the old picnic table?"

The old picnic table has an awning, but it doesn't offer much shade and it doesn't have a good view of the soccer practice. But at least it's something to do. Marisol walks over to the table, but instead of sitting on the bench, she lies on the table and holds Pot Roast overhead. She practices throwing Pot Roast high in the air and catching him. The picnic table is scratchy under her back. Beads of sweat trickle around her ears.

The sounds of her brother's soccer practice sail toward her. Some of his teammates are chanting "Oz-zie! Oz-zie!" That's what they do when he's being extraordinary.

"Oz is an extraordinary athlete!" people say, again and again. Oz's soccer coach. Oz's gym teacher at school. Oz's friends' parents. Even Dadhead, and he only gets to see Oz play every now and then.

Marisol wants to be an extraordinary something.

She decides to travel far, far away, in her imagination. She's going to a different world. A world where she is *extraordinary*. She imagines that she's playing a game, just like Oz. Maybe it's kickball. Maybe it's soccer. Maybe it's basketball. The point is: She is the best one on the entire

team, and no one can believe how extraordinary
she is. Not even Evie Smythe, who is the most
shocked of all.

Here's the best part: Coach Decker is there. And he doesn't say, "Nice try, Marisol!" or "Great effort, Marisol!" Instead, he says . . .

That makes Marisol happy, even if it's just in her imagination.

NOT FAIR

In gym class on Thursday, Coach Decker puts them in pairs again for their next set of drills. This time, they practice catching. Coach Decker says they should stand close together and toss the ball back and forth. They're supposed to add a little space after each throw so they can learn to catch and throw from a greater and greater distance. This is to practice for the outfield.

Marisol makes sure that she and Felix stand far away from Evie this time. Instead, they're next to Jada and Sherry Roat. Sherry is good at all the sports, just like Evie, but she doesn't brag about it. Sherry has a blond ponytail that she wears right on top of her head, and she always has extra pencils and paper if you forget yours. Sherry and Marisol were partners in gym last year, when they were jumping rope. Sherry was a good partner.

Felix is a good partner, too.

"Is it true you can talk to animals?" Jada asks Felix as she catches Sherry's toss.

It's not as noisy as it was when they practiced kicking.

"Yep," Felix says. He throws the ball to Marisol.

Marisol catches it and asks, "How?"

"Yeah," says Sherry. "How?"

"Do the animals talk to you *out loud*?" asks

Jada. She doesn't say it in a mean way, but Marisol knows Jada doesn't totally believe Felix.

Marisol isn't sure if she does, either.

"No. It's in my mind." Felix taps his forehead. "Like, I can sense what they're saying."

Felix takes a step back, as Coach Decker said. Marisol does, too, but only a small one, like an inch. That way she's not breaking the rules, but she's not putting much distance between them, either. What if Felix gets too far away and she can't catch the ball?

"How did you find out you could do it?" Marisol asks. She tosses the ball back to Felix.

"Well," Felix begins, his face brightening. "One day, I was sitting there with Mary Puppins, and I—"

"Who?" Sherry interrupts.

"Mary Puppins," Felix says. "My dog."

Marisol smiles. It's a good name.

"What kind of dog is it?" Jada asks.

"We don't know. We got her from a rescue."

"Is it a big dog or a little dog?" Marisol asks.

"A little dog."

Sherry tilts her head. "*How* little, though?"

"Like, the size of a chihuahua," Felix says.

"Does it have long hair or short hair?" Jada asks.

"Short hair." Felix sighs. "Do you want to hear how I learned to talk to animals or not?"

Mary Puppins

The girls nod.

"Okay," Felix says. "Here's how it happened. My parents got me a book called *Animal* for my birthday. It's a big, thick book, like the thickest book you can imagine." He tosses the kickball to Marisol and indicates the size of the book with his hands. Marisol barely catches the ball this time— and when she does, she drops it. Thankfully, no one notices. "It has everything you ever wanted to know about all kinds of animals," Felix continues. "I read it in bed every night."

Marisol throws the ball back to Felix. He catches it without even looking.

"One morning, I woke up and I was sleeping with my head on the book, like it was a pillow," he says. "Mary Puppins was there and she looked at me and I knew exactly what she was thinking."

"What was she thinking?" Marisol asks, wide eyed.

"She was thinking, 'I want a dog treat.' In those *exact* words," Felix says. "All the stuff from the book must have gone into my brain while I was asleep. Now I'm, like, an animal expert."

Jada raises one eyebrow. "That sounds suspicious."

Felix shrugs with one shoulder and takes another step back. "It's true. I got her a dog treat and she said thank you."

"I don't believe you," Sherry says.

"I'm telling you, it's true," Felix says. He turns to Marisol. "Do you believe me, Marisol?"

He throws the kickball to her.

Marisol isn't sure how to answer, but it doesn't matter, because she misses the ball completely this time. It sails by her head and *bounce, bounce, bounces* across the gym. Marisol runs after it. She feels like there's a bright spotlight on her the whole time. She is the first person to miss a catch.

It's all because Felix was standing too far away, Marisol tells herself. When she gets back with the ball, she's angry at Felix. She's even a little angry at Jada and Sherry. All the conversation about Mary Puppins was distracting.

Besides, humans can't talk to animals, right? Surely *everyone* knows that!

Marisol throws the ball to Felix and doesn't say anything for the rest of gym.

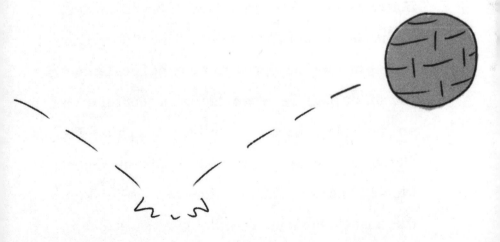

RIGHT NOWS
AND WHAT-IFS

It's eleven o'clock at night, and Marisol is wide-awake. There are times when she is the only person awake in the whole house. It's all because of the Brain Train. When Marisol can't sleep, she lies in bed and stares at the ceiling. Sometimes she sneaks into Oz's room to watch silent movies on his laptop. Lately, she's been watching *The Circus*, which is on her List of Favorite Silent Movies. Marisol loves old silent movies, the kind they made more than a hundred years ago, before they knew how to record sound. They're funny, even though no one talks.

But she doesn't want to get up right now. She wants to stay where she is, with Beans and all her stuffed animals nearby. One of the thoughts that pops into her head is: *If my dad were here, he could teach me to play kickball.*

Mrs. Rainey is terrible at sports, just like Marisol. But not Mr. Rainey. Back when Mr. Rainey was a teenager, he played baseball. And if he were here, he and Marisol could practice in the backyard. Then she wouldn't have to worry so much.

The thought grows and grows, and then she's mad.

Why does Dadhead have to work so far away and be gone all the time?

It isn't fair.

The Brain Train chugs and chugs. It's exhausting sometimes.

Marisol decides to focus on something else to slow everything down. She closes her eyes and feels the tickle of Beans's tail against her arm. The plushiness of Nacho and Lumpia. The *hum-hum-hum* of her overhead fan.

"Sometimes it helps to focus on the right nows so you don't get lost in the what-ifs," Ms. Ruby said once to the class.

It works, mostly. The train slows down, and now Marisol is thinking about Felix and how she never answered his question. She's worried she hurt his feelings. But she's still not sure whether she believes him or not. She's pretty sure he's making it up, but he doesn't seem like the type of person who tells lies.

If he can really talk to animals, Marisol thinks, *maybe I can, too.*

Marisol would love to talk to animals. She has plenty of things to say to them.

Who knows? Maybe Felix *is* telling the truth. And if so, maybe he'll teach her how to do it. If she could talk to animals, she wouldn't care so much about kickball. She'd just run into the forest and talk to woodland creatures all day. Once she found a forest, that is.

Tomorrow, she will gather evidence to find out whether Felix is telling the truth. And if he is, she will ask him to show her how to talk to animals, too.

Surely he will agree to that.

ACCORDING TO FELIX

When Marisol wakes up on Friday, she thinks about kickball first and Felix second. At school, Marisol sees kickballs everywhere. There are kickballs in math. There are kickballs in science. There are kickballs in social studies. Today is Friday, and their first game isn't until Tuesday, which means Marisol has several days to worry.

She decides to focus—or *try* to focus—on Felix
instead. She tells Jada the plan to gather evidence
on whether or not Felix is telling the truth.

"How are you going to do that?" asks Jada as
they head outside for recess. Sherry is walking
with them, too.

Marisol pats her tote bag, the one with a cat wearing sunglasses on it. She only brings it to school for special occasions, like today. "I brought Pot Roast to school," Marisol says.

Sherry raises her eyebrows. "But we just ate lunch. And what does pot roast have to do with anything?"

"But Pot Roast won't work," says Jada to Marisol. "We need Beans. Beans would be better."

They walk out into the bright afternoon. Clusters of kids rush to the monkey bars and jungle gym and basketball court.

"Why do we need beans?" asks Sherry. "I don't even like beans!"

"Pot Roast is one of Marisol's stuffed animals. He's a cat," Jada explains. "Beans is also a cat, but he's real. *Not* stuffed."

"I have a real-life cat, too," Sherry says. "His name is Mr. Whiskers."

Marisol scans the playground for Felix and sees him near the slides. She makes a beeline for him, with Sherry and Jada by her side. He looks up when they approach and runs toward them.

"Wanna play Food Tag?" he says.

"Maybe later," Marisol replies. "We want to test your skills first."

Felix frowns. "My Food Tag skills? I'm great at Food Tag. Everyone knows I'm the *master chef* of Food Tag."

"No, not that," Jada says. She crosses her arms. "Your animal-talking skills."

Jada thinks Felix is making everything up, but Marisol wants to give him the benefit of the doubt.

"Oh, those," Felix says casually. "Okay. But how?"

He looks around, as if searching for nearby animals. But there are too many loud, screaming kids on the playground. He motions toward the big oak tree.

"I could try to get Reginald," he suggests.

It's a good idea, but Marisol doesn't want to go anywhere near the Big Tree, because that's where Evie is at this very moment.

"I have a better idea." Marisol reaches into her tote bag and pulls out Pot Roast. "This is Pot Roast."

Felix raises one eyebrow. "That's a stuffed animal."

"Duh," Sherry says.

"You can use Pot Roast to show us *how* you do it," Marisol says.

"But that won't prove anything," Jada says. "He could make it all up. We need real evidence."

Jada's parents are both professors at the university, so she knows about things like evidence and democracy. Sometimes Jada even *sounds* like a professor. But Marisol has already thought her plan through.

"If Felix shows *us* how to do it, then we can test it on our own," Marisol explains. "I can try it on Beans, and Sherry can try it on Mr. Whiskers. Then we can report our findings."

Jada scrunches up her mouth, thinking. Then she nods. "Okay. Good plan."

"Is it something you can teach us, or is it, like, a superpower or something?" Sherry asks as Felix leads them to a shaded spot near the library windows.

"I can *try* to teach you, but I don't know if it will work or not," he says. "Maybe it's something only I can do. A natural talent!"

Felix heard that phrase from Ms. Ruby. Marisol knows this because she heard Ms. Ruby use the term "natural talent" before, too. Like when Isabella Sanchez sang "The Star-Spangled Banner" for an assembly or when Lucas Richardson drew a perfect isosceles triangle on the whiteboard in math, Ms. Ruby said they had "natural talent."

Marisol isn't sure what her natural talent is, but maybe it's talking to animals, like Felix, or gathering evidence, like she's doing right now.

Sherry, Marisol, Jada, and Felix sit in a circle with Pot Roast in the middle.

Felix lowers his voice. "Okay," he says. "Here's how it works."

How to talk to ANimaLs...

#1. Study them closely.

#2. Imagine wHat it's Like to Be them.

#3. Block everything out of your mind and concentrate.

#4. Start a conversation.

How was your day, Mary Puppins?

That's enough conversation. Time for treats.

As soon as Felix finishes explaining his process, the bell rings. Marisol puts Pot Roast back in her tote bag as he rushes off. Felix always likes to be at the head of the line.

"I'll try it with Mr. Whiskers this weekend," Sherry says.

Marisol nods. "I'll try it with Beans, too."

They stand up and brush themselves off. Jada doesn't say anything.

"What do you think, Jada?" Marisol asks.

"I don't have any pets," Jada says. She frowns. "I don't even have Cornelius."

Marisol knows what it's like to miss something that you don't have. Especially something as important as Cornelius.

Marisol slips her tote bag off her shoulder and gives it to Jada.

"Pot Roast can keep you company until Cornelius comes back," Marisol says.

Jada's face brightens. She hugs Pot Roast to her chest.

"Gracias," Jada says, which means "thank you" in Spanish.

DADHEAD

When Dadhead calls that night, Marisol doesn't feel like talking. There is a tight knot in the center of her belly, because she's been thinking about how unfair it is that her dad is so far away when she needs him. If he were here, he could help her practice kickball in the backyard. Instead, he's way out in the Gulf of Mexico.

Even worse, Oz is talking endlessly about his upcoming soccer game.

"We got a text saying that the game might get

canceled because of rain. I'll be *so mad* if we don't get to play, because I'm ready to demolish the Chargers," Oz is saying to Dadhead. His knee is bouncing under the table because he's so excited. "They have this forward who thinks he's the next Cristiano Ronaldo or something."

"Oz," Mrs. Rainey says. "That's not very nice."

Oz shrugs and picks up his phone. Marisol doesn't have a phone, because her parents say she's not old enough. And she docsn't have a laptop yet, either. And she doesn't have a dad to teach her how to play kickball.

The knot tightens and tightens.

"There's supposed to be a storm coming, but you never know," Dadhead says. "Things change minute to minute."

Dadhead leans forward and looks at Marisol. Marisol usually worries about Dadhead when storms blow through, even though he's explained that oil rigs are very strong and can withstand lots of rain and wind. If she didn't have the knot in her belly, she might worry right now. But she's too focused on the fact that he's *there* and not *here*.

"What's the matter, Scraps?" he says. "You look unhappy."

Marisol decides to confess how worried she is about kickball. She doesn't even care if Oz makes fun of her. But just as she opens her mouth, Oz's phone chimes. It's his best friend, Stu, who also happens to be Evie Smythe's older brother. Oz answers, even though Dadhead and Marisol are in the middle of a conversation, which Marisol thinks is rude.

"Go in the other room if you're going to talk on the phone," Mrs. Rainey says.

Oz holds the phone away from his face and waves at Dadhead. "Later, Dad," Oz says.

"Later, Ronaldo," Dadhead says.

Now is Marisol's chance to tell Dadhead what's bothering her, but Dadhead starts talking about something else. He forgot he asked the question.

Marisol leans back in her chair with Nacho and doesn't say a word.

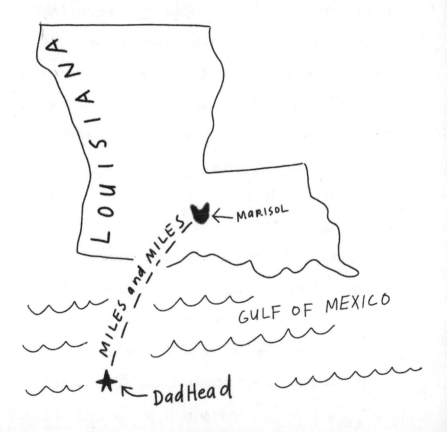

HEADSPACE

Sometimes a good dinner can make you feel better, but that night Mrs. Rainey makes pork chops and macaroni and cheese. Pork chops are nowhere on Marisol's List of Favorite Foods. She has two helpings of macaroni and cheese and takes tiny bites of her pork chop so it looks like she at least tried to eat it. By the time she goes to bed, she's hungry again and secretly wishes she could eat even more macaroni. Or maybe a big bowl of vanilla ice cream with lots of chocolate on top. And sprinkles. And peanuts.

Instead, she sits cross-legged on her cat comforter and looks at Beans. He is curled into a tight ball on Marisol's bed, but he's not asleep. Marisol studies his face—his whiskers, the patterns on his fur, the shape of his little black nose—then she rushes to her dresser (which she has named Mabel) to grab a pair of cat ears. She puts them on and climbs back on the bed.

Marisol closes her eyes and tries to imagine what it's like to be Beans. What does he see when he walks around the house? What does he smell? What does he think? What makes him happy? What makes him *unhappy*?

My FAVORITE ThiNgs
By Beans

1. TREATS
2. BeLLy RuBS
3. Snacks
4. Head RuBS
5. DinneR

When Marisol opens her eyes, Beans is asleep. She isn't sure if it's possible to talk to animals while they're sleeping, but it's worth a try. That's something she'll have to ask Felix.

"Beans?" Marisol whispers.

She waits for an answer—even just a plain old meow—but Beans doesn't make a sound. He just keeps sleeping. Marisol wonders what he's dreaming about.

There is a knock on her bedroom door and Mrs. Rainey pokes her head in, holding her phone.

"Dad wanted to talk to you one last time before he goes to bed," Mrs. Rainey says. She comes in and sits next to Marisol. Beans opens his eyes, stretches, and goes back to sleep.

Marisol takes her mother's phone and sees Dadhead on the screen. He's not in the mess hall anymore. It looks like he's in his bunk. The beds on the oil rig aren't very comfortable, but Dadhead says he's used to it.

"Hey, Scraps," Dadhead says.

"Hey, Dad," says Marisol.

"I wanted to check on you one last time," Dadhead says. "Everything okay?"

Marisol isn't sure if she wants to tell Dadhead about her kickball problem after all. If she were to tell the whole truth and nothing but the truth, she would say: *We are playing kickball in gym next week and I'm really worried because I know I won't be good at kickball and I'm going to let my whole team down and they'll all see how terrible I am. I wish I was an extraordinary athlete like Oz. But I'm not. I'm just Marisol.*

But that feels like a lot of words to say all at once,

so she says instead, "We're playing kickball in gym next week, and I'm not good at kickball." She pauses, then adds, "I wish you were here to teach me."

Mrs. Rainey reaches over and squeezes Marisol's shoulder, which makes Marisol feel a little better.

"Me, too," Dadhead says.

"I wish I was a great athlete like Oz," Marisol says quietly.

Dadhead smiles. "You don't have to be anyone but Marisol. Marisol is wonderful just as she is."

Beans rolls over onto his back. Marisol rubs his belly.

"You could ask Oz to help you practice," Dadhead says.

Marisol scrunches up her nose. She's not sure if that's a good idea. What if he makes fun of her?

"Maybe," Marisol says. "Maybe."

QUEENS

It's cloudy on the day of Oz's soccer game, but it doesn't rain. Oz scores two goals. The Tornadoes win—four to three—and Mrs. Rainey takes them to Armijo's for ice cream to celebrate. But they're getting it to go, so Mrs. Rainey doesn't let Marisol order a banana split. She says it's too messy to eat in the car. Marisol settles for a cup of vanilla with rainbow sprinkles.

When they get home, Oz immediately snatches a bag of chips out of the pantry and rushes to his room to play *Knights of Redemption*, his favorite video game. He doesn't even take a shower, even though he really, *really* smells, and he doesn't even wash his hands, which are sticky from soft serve.

Marisol washes hers, though. Then she borrows her mother's phone and calls Jada. She wants Jada to come over so they can practice for the kickball game. Marisol also plans to take her father's advice and ask Oz for help. Jada agrees that it's a good idea, even if she thinks Oz is generally gross and annoying.

As soon as Jada arrives, she and Marisol march upstairs and knock on Oz's door.

"What!" he yells.

Marisol opens the door and pokes her head in. As suspected, Oz is sitting on his bean bag chair, wearing headphones, still in his soccer uniform, with a bag of Doritos next to him. He doesn't look away from his screen, where medieval knights swing swords at his command.

"What do you want?" he says when Marisol doesn't say anything.

"We need your help," says Marisol.

Oz's room really stinks. Gross! Marisol pinches her nose.

"What?" shouts Oz. He can't hear because his game is so loud.

"We need your help," Marisol repeats. Her voice sounds funny because her nose is pinched, and Jada laughs. Marisol tries not to laugh but starts to giggle. That's the thing about best friends—laughing is contagious.

Oz pauses the game, pulls off his headphones, and turns to her. "You need *what?*"

"We need your help!" Marisol and Jada yell at the same time.

"Help with what?"

Marisol and Jada exchange looks. They're both pinching their noses now. Marisol releases hers.

"We need you to make us kickball queens," she says.

THE ULTIMATE RULE
OF KICKBALL

Marisol and Jada stand side by side in the backyard after Oz agrees to help them. Oz faces them from a few feet away. He's holding the soccer ball in front of him like a precious gem. Luckily, the sky is still packed with clouds so it's not unbearably hot outside. There's even a slight breeze. Marisol can hear birds chirping in the distance.

"The ultimate rule of kickball—the ultimate rule of any kind of ball game, actually—is simple,"

Oz begins. His hair is still sweaty and stuck to his forehead. "If you remember this one rule, you will always be ready."

Marisol and Jada stare at him, wide-eyed.

"Are you ready to hear the rule?" Oz asks.

They nod.

"Do you promise to abide by this rule to the best of your ability at all times?" Oz asks.

They nod.

"Do you understand the *importance* of the ultimate rule of kickball?" Oz asks.

They nod.

"Okay," Oz says. He pauses. "The ultimate rule is"—his face turns serious—*"Never take your eye off the ball."*

He moves the soccer ball to the left and to the right to make sure they follow it with their eyes. Left. Right. Left. Right. They do.

"Repeat after me," he says. He clears his throat. *"Never."*

"Never."

He moves the ball slightly to the right. *"Take."*

"Take," they say, following the ball with their eyes.

"Your."

"Your."

He moves the ball slightly to the left. *"Eye."*

They follow the ball. "Eye."

"Off."

"Off."

"The." He raises the ball over his head.

"The." Their eyes follow.

"Ball."

"Ball."

Oz drops the soccer ball at his feet. Marisol and Jada watch it fall, then stare at him, waiting for what happens next. He raises his arms and slaps them down at his sides.

"Why are you looking at *me*?" he says. "I *just* told you to never take your eye off the ball!"

Marisol and Jada mumble apologies and refocus as Oz takes a few steps back. He tells them to spread apart so he can kick it to one of them. Then they're supposed to kick it back.

"And don't forget the ultimate rule this time," he says.

"Which one of us are you going to kick it to?" Jada asks as she and Marisol put space between them.

Oz sighs. "I'm not going to *tell* you."

"Why not?" Marisol asks.

"Yeah," Jada agrees. "Why not? If you tell us, we can be ready."

"That's the whole point," Oz says. "If I'm on the other team, I don't want you to be ready. I want you to be the opposite of ready. That's why you have to be on high alert and *never take your eye off the ball.*"

"What if we need to throw it to someone?" Jada asks. "How are we supposed to throw it to someone if we can't look at them?"

Oz puts his hands on top of his head and releases a super-exasperated groan.

"Let's just focus on kicking right now, okay?" he says.

Jada shrugs.

Oz takes a running start—as Evie would call it—and Marisol keeps her eyes on the ball, just as he said. There's a soft *thwap* sound when he kicks it, which makes her jump, because she's worried it might sail through the air and knock her over. Instead, it glides gently toward Jada, who kicks it back on the first try.

"Awesome!" says Oz. He stops the ball with his foot.

Jada claps. Marisol does, too. But she stops clapping when she realizes that Oz is kicking the ball again, right in her direction. She keeps her eye on it and even raises her foot to kick it, but she misses. The ball rolls to the fence behind her, then stops.

"Don't worry about it," Oz says. "We'll try again. That's why it's called practice."

Marisol picks up the soccer ball and throws it to Oz, but it doesn't go very far. He has to jog a few steps to retrieve it. Marisol is embarrassed, even though you shouldn't feel embarrassed in front of best friends and brothers. She wishes she didn't feel embarrassed. She wishes she didn't feel jealous of Jada for kicking it perfectly on the first try. She wishes she didn't have a knot in her belly about the kickball game.

But sometimes you can't help how you feel.

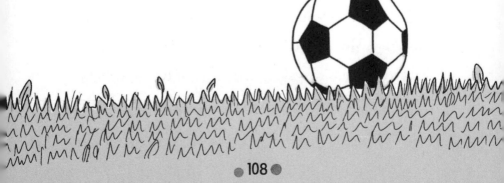

NOT ONE DROP

"I've been talking to Mr. Whiskers for three days, and he hasn't communicated with me at all," Sherry Roat says.

It's Tuesday, and Sherry, Jada, and Marisol are walking toward the gym in a single-file line with the rest of the class. They aren't supposed to talk in line, but Sherry is going on and on about Mr. Whiskers. Marisol isn't completely listening. She's distracted because today is the first of two kickball games, and her heart is beating in her chest.

The practice with Oz wasn't a total disaster. Marisol missed lots of kicks, but she made just as many. And she even learned how to throw a little bit better. *And* she caught all of Oz's throws.

Well. *Almost* all of them.

Marisol should feel prepared. Jada does. Jada says she isn't that worried about kickball anymore because Oz showed them how easy and fun it is. Surely, at the very least, they'll be able to kick the ball.

Surely.

"Maybe Mr. Whiskers is the quiet type," Jada says. "What do you think, Marisol?"

Marisol shrugs because she doesn't know how to respond, and because she doesn't want to break the rule about talking in line. It doesn't matter, anyway, because now they're at the gym

So anyway then Ms. Ruby said I had really good handwriting that's when I decided to practice calligraphy But it was a lot more work than I thought plus the pens were really messy But maybe I should keep practicing, what do you think, Mr. Whiskers, I mean you may not have an opinion since you're a cat but maybe you do, I mean, who knows? But if I have such good penmanship I don't think I should let it go to waste so I don't know but anyway

Sherry →

← Mr. Whiskers

and Coach Decker is standing there with a big smile plastered on his face.

"Welcome, kickballers!" he shouts. He has a bag of kickballs at his feet. He motions for them to gather around, which they all do.

Some of the kids cheer. Felix cheers. Isabella cheers. Lucas cheers. But Evie Smythe cheers the loudest. Evie wore special sneakers today, specifically for kickball, and she was all too happy to show them to everyone at recess.

Marisol does not cheer. She is standing by Sherry, Jada, and Felix and wishing she didn't feel so nervous. No one else looks nervous. Why does she have to be the only one?

"Today is our first kickball game!" Coach Decker says.

Everyone cheers again.

Marisol wishes he'd quit talking in exclamation points.

"First things first," he continues. "The rules of kickball—"

"I already know the rules, Coach Decker!" Evie chimes in.

Jada sticks out her tongue, but only Marisol sees. She tries not to giggle.

"—are very similar to baseball," Coach Decker

goes on. "The biggest difference is, you can't strike out in our version of kickball. When it's your turn 'to bat,' you kick until you hit the ball. No strikeouts!"

He picks up the bag of kickballs and throws it over his shoulder. "Let's go!" he says. As the students follow him obediently to the field outside, Evie leans over to Marisol.

"No strikeouts," Evie says. "Lucky for you, Marisol!"

"Shows how much you know, Evie!" Jada hisses with her face scrunched up tight. "Marisol is a *great* kickballer! She could be a *professional* kickballer, if she really wanted!"

"Yeah!" Sherry says, in agreement.

"HA!" snorts Evie, before jogging off toward Coach Decker.

Marisol doesn't know what to say. Part of her

is happy that her best friend stood up for her, but part of her feels like Jada shouldn't have said that, because now the knot inside her belly is tighter than ever.

Marisol looks toward the sky.

It's still cloudy.

It's been cloudy for days with no rain.

Marisol wishes for a thunderstorm. She wishes the sky would crack open and sheets of rain would fall. She imagines Coach Decker rushing them all back inside, where they hula-hoop or run races. She imagines it with all her might.

Please rain. Please rain. Please rain.

But it doesn't.

Not one drop.

THE ANGRY SEED

When the group reaches the baseball diamond for their very first kickball game, Coach Decker drops the bag of kickballs. The grass is dry and crunchy under Marisol's sneakers. In science, Marisol learned that rain is good for the environment because it helps things grow. Now she has two reasons to wish for a thunderstorm—the grass would get something to drink, and she wouldn't have to play kickball.

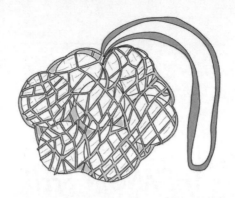

Coach Decker announces that he's going to separate them into ones and twos. Marisol's heart plummets. She is standing right next to Jada, which means there's no way they'll be on the same team. Sure enough, Coach points an index finger at each of them in turn, counting off "One! Two! One! Two!" Marisol is a *one.* Jada is a *two.*

"Boo!" Jada grumbles.

Coach tells the *ones* to go into the outfield. The *twos* will start as kickers. He points to the different parts of the field where they're supposed to go—right, left, and center. That's when Marisol realizes that Evie is on her team, too. So is Sherry.

"Great," Evie says to Sherry. "Marisol is on our team. Now we'll never win."

"Marisol is a great kickballer, just like Jada said," Sherry says. "Just wait. You'll see."

Marisol knows Sherry is trying to help, but she wishes she hadn't said that.

Evie goes to first base. Sherry goes to second. Marisol doesn't want to be on a base. She doesn't want to be anywhere, but she *really* doesn't want to be on a base. She walks to the outfield, as far as she can go before Coach Decker tells her to stop. *Surely no one will kick a ball this far,* Marisol thinks. *Surely not.*

But she's wrong.

Felix kicks the ball on the first try, and it sails right toward Marisol. Evie yells "Catch it! Catch it!" because if you catch a ball before it hits the ground, it counts as an out. But Marisol doesn't catch it. The ball thuds to the ground near her feet. She scrambles to pick it up and rears her arms back the way Oz taught her, but Marisol isn't sure where she should throw it. Should she throw it to first base or home? She doesn't know. And as she thinks it over, Felix runs all the way to second. Marisol aims the ball at Sherry and throws, but the ball doesn't go very far. It lands on the grass and rolls toward Sherry, who picks it up and tosses it to Isabella, the pitcher.

Thankfully, the ball doesn't go near Marisol again—not even when Jada kicks it and makes a home run. It's the first home run of the game, and everyone cheers and cheers, and Coach Decker gives Jada double high-fives and shouts, "Way to go, Jada! Way to go!"

Marisol knows she should be happy for her best friend. Jada's smile is huge and brightens her whole face. Jada looks very proud, and Marisol knows that's a good thing. But a little part of her is angry and mad. It's like there's a tiny seed buried in her chest, and the seed is full of mean things, like jealousy. The tiny seed says things like: Jada has never been good at sports before. Why does she have to be good *right now*, when Marisol is so terrible?

When it's time for the teams to switch, Marisol thinks, *Maybe I'll hit a home run, too. After all, I practiced with Oz, just like Jada. If Jada can hit a home run, surely I can. Right?*

She doesn't believe it—not totally and completely, with her whole heart—but it's possible, right?

Anything is possible.

Right?

Angry Seed

BITE

Marisol does not hit a home run.

Marisol misses the first pitch. The ball sails right by her raised foot and directly to Lucas, who is the catcher. Marisol is the only person to miss one of the pitches. No one has to tell her this—she already knows.

Marisol kicks the ball on the second try, but it's as if her foot is deflated and defeated, and the ball barely goes anywhere. Lucas immediately picks it up and taps her on the shoulder. She doesn't even make it halfway to the base before she's out. When she walks off to the sidelines, Evie rolls her eyes at her and shakes her head.

Coach Decker told them they weren't keeping score, since they were just "playing for fun," but Marisol didn't have fun, and she knows that her team didn't win. Everyone does. The angry seed in her chest grows and grows. She's mad at herself. She's mad at Oz for not being a better teacher. She's mad at Dadhead for not being around to help her. And she's even mad at Jada. After the game, she doesn't want to talk to Jada or anyone else.

"I can't believe I got a home run!" Jada says as she, Marisol, and Sherry get in line.

"It was amazing!" Sherry says.

Now Marisol is mad at Sherry, because they're

supposed to be on the same team.

Evie is making her way into line, too. "I knew Jada didn't know what she was talking about," she says. "Unless 'professional kickball player,' meant 'worst player on the whole planet'!"

Marisol narrows her eyes at Evie, but doesn't say anything, because Coach Decker is right there. But the seed growls and growls in her chest, and she wants to let it bite.

She turns to Jada, who is standing behind her.

"The only reason you got a home run is because *my brother* taught you how to play," Marisol whispers.

Jada's smile disappears.

Marisol thought it would make her feel better to snap at Jada, but it doesn't.

She only feels worse.

MEOW FOR YES

Marisol didn't feel better by Wednesday afternoon. She didn't feel better after practicing with Oz again in the backyard. She didn't feel better after talking to Dadhead. She didn't feel better after taking a bath, brushing her hair, and putting on her favorite kitten pajamas. She's mad at herself for hurting Jada's feelings. She still hasn't apologized, and she's mad at herself for that, too. She opened her mouth to say "I'm sorry" a bunch of times, but it wouldn't come out. Jada doesn't seem upset anymore, but surely Marisol should apologize—right?

To make matters worse, tomorrow is Thursday again, which means there's another kickball game.

Next week, kickball will be over. You would think this would make Marisol feel better, but it doesn't. She wants to skip right over Thursday and go straight to Friday.

WEDNESDAY / THURSDAY / FRIDAY /

She wishes she had a fast-forward button, but she doesn't.

She does have a plan, though. Sort of.

For one thing, she has secretly snatched Oz's soccer ball and brought it to her room. She placed it next to her pillow after wiping it down and wrapping it in a towel. That's where it sits right now. The bed is a bit crowded with the soccer ball, Beans, Lumpia, Nacho, Banana Split, and Hi-C, but it's worth the sacrifice. Pot Roast is still having a sleepover at Jada's, so that gives everyone slightly more wiggle room.

If Felix can learn to communicate with animals by sleeping on a big, thick book, maybe Marisol can learn how to kick and run the bases by snuggling with the soccer ball.

Well, she won't *snuggle,* exactly. It's difficult to snuggle a soccer ball.

The second part of Marisol's plan is to wish, wish, wish that it rains tomorrow. She's going to wish with all her might. She's going to wish harder than anyone has ever wished before. There are supposed to be scattered thunderstorms this week, according to Dadhead. And if it rains, the game will be canceled, which is almost as good as skipping over Thursday altogether.

She closes her eyes and concentrates.

Please make it rain tomorrow.

Please make it rain tomorrow.

Please make it rain tomorrow.

She repeats this over and over. She imagines the wishes traveling through the air and into the universe, drifting all the way to the rain clouds and making them so heavy that they'll eventually have to rain . . . but only when it's time for gym class and not a minute before or after.

Surely it couldn't hurt to send wishes into the air—right?

At some point Beans crawls onto the pillow
next to Marisol and curls up by her face. Marisol
feels the tickle of his fur. She opens one eye.

"Beans?" she says.

Beans has never slept next to her head.

"Are you okay?" Marisol asks.

Beans meows.

Marisol opens both eyes.

Maybe Beans is just meowing. But what if it's more than a meow?

What if he's *communicating*?

"Do you think it will rain tomorrow?" she whispers. "Meow for yes."

Beans doesn't meow. He licks his front paw and purrs.

"Do you think I'm a terrible best friend?" she asks. "Meow for yes."

Beans stops licking his paw and lifts his head. He looks at Marisol, but doesn't make a sound.

Marisol stares at Beans. "Do you think I'll be extraordinary at the kickball game tomorrow?" she whispers.

Beans yawns.

He lays down his head.

And meows.

STILL BEST FRIENDS

The next day, there's an announcement over the speaker that recess will be indoors because there's a chance of rain. Indoor recess means they have to go to the gym, where everyone's voices bounce off the floor and walls, making it super loud. Marisol doesn't usually like places that are super loud, but when you have the right friends, you can make a cocoon. When you have a perfect best-friend cocoon, it feels like no one else matters. Marisol and Jada make today's cocoon behind the basketball hoop, where Jada reaches into her backpack and pulls out Marisol's tote bag and Pot Roast.

"I'm going to my dad's tomorrow, so you can have Pot Roast back," Jada says. "Thanks for letting her stay with me."

Marisol is very happy to see Pot Roast. Even though she trusts Jada, it's hard being away from someone you love. Before Marisol takes Pot Roast, though, she decides to apologize.

"I'm sorry I snapped at you after you got your home run," Marisol says quietly. "I was just jealous."

"Lo so," Jada replies, which means "I know" in Italian. She sighs. "I'm sorry I told Evie you could be a professional kickballer."

"It's okay," Marisol says. "You were trying to help."

Jada smiles wide—almost as wide as when

she got her home run. "Still best friends?"

Marisol nods. "Still best friends."

Jada gives Pot Roast one last, long hug and then places her in Marisol's lap.

MARISOL STEPS UP
TO THE PLATE

When it's time for the kickball game, Marisol hopes with all her might that Coach Decker will be standing in the center of the gym with the bins full of hula hoops and paddleballs. She imagines him sighing sadly and saying, "Unfortunately, we have to cancel our kickball game today because of the rain." Maybe Marisol will sigh, too, and pretend like she's disappointed.

But as soon as she walks into the gym, Marisol sees Coach Decker, holding the big net bag of kickballs. He tells them to follow him outside, and she does. She walks as slowly as possible. Surely the longer it takes for them to get to the field, the better. She moves so slowly that Jada and Sherry are soon several steps ahead as Marisol straggles in the back, like a caboose that's almost unhinged from the train.

Felix sees her and comes her way.

"Hey, Marisol," he says. "Did you try talking to Beans?"

"Yep," Marisol says.

"Did it work?"

"I'm not sure," Marisol says. "I asked him three questions and told him to meow for yes."

"Did he meow?"

"Yes. But how am I supposed to know if he was saying yes or if he was just meowing?"

"Well, that depends," Felix says. Marisol can tell that he wants to walk faster, but he's staying in step with her. "What did you ask him?"

Marisol feels her cheeks warm slightly with embarrassment. She doesn't want to tell Felix what she asked Beans.

"I just asked how my day would go today," she says. Marisol doesn't like telling lies, but it's sort of the truth, right?

"Well, when the day's over, you'll know if he was really talking or just meowing," Felix says. He takes off running before she can respond, which is fine with Marisol, because she wants to mentally review Oz's tips for playing kickball—especially the ultimate rule. Marisol eyes the kickball field, which gets closer with every step.

Despite her best efforts, she arrives at the diamond.

Marisol's team is assigned to the field first.

Marisol stands in her usual spot, hoping the ball doesn't come her way. Every now and then she glances at the sky, waiting for the thunderstorm, but mostly she follows Oz's ultimate rule and focuses on the ball. She's concentrating so hard that she almost doesn't hear Evie Smythe's screechy voice or Coach Decker's whistle. She's focusing so hard that she doesn't realize it's time for the teams to switch sides.

She exhales as they jog off the field.

At least the ball never came her way. Surely that's something.

When they line up as kickers, Evie pushes herself way ahead of everyone so she's first.

Marisol goes to the back of the line. When she gets close to the front, she tries to sneak to the back again, but it doesn't work. Too many people are watching, including Coach Decker.

The line ahead of her gets shorter as each player goes up to kick. There are no strikes. So far, Marisol is the only one who's made a strike in kickball at Getty Elementary School. Everyone else kicks the ball with no problem. *Thwack!* Evie's ball sailed through the air, and she made

it all the way to second base. *Thwack!* Sherry makes it to third. *Thwack! Thwack! Thwack!*

Marisol can hear her heartbeat in her ears. She wants to sneak to the back of the line again, but Coach Decker is paying attention. When it's her turn to step to the plate, she has no choice but to go.

"Don't strike out, Marisol!" says Evie, squeezing her mouth in a disapproving knot.

Marisol stands back from the plate so she can get a running start.

She wipes her hands on her shorts.

At first she has her eyes on Felix, the pitcher, because she wants to send him a telepathic message that says *Please roll the ball slowly and straight toward my foot.* But then she remembers Oz's ultimate rule.

She locks her eyes on the ball.

She watches as Felix pulls it back.

She watches as he releases it.

She watches it roll, roll, roll toward her feet.

She takes a few steps toward it. She tries not to think too hard.

She keeps her eye on the ball.

Thwack!

The last time she played kickball, she barely felt the ball hit her foot. This time, she does. It's the best *thwack* she's ever heard, and it moves through her leg. And now she's running. She's running as fast as she can to first base!

The ball doesn't sail as far as it did when Evie or Sherry kicked it, but it goes far enough. Marisol stops, looks down, and sees first base under her sneakers. Then she looks up and sees

Jada cheering for her in the outfield, even though she's on the opposite team.

Guess who else is clapping?

Evie Smythe.

And Coach Decker.

"Way to go, Marisol!" he shouts. "Way to go!"

Marisol feels lighter than the kickball, like she can fly into the air. She wants to clap, but she's not sure if it's okay to cheer for yourself or not. She decides it is. She claps, but only three times. Clap. Clap. Clap.

Beans was right, Marisol thinks.

She is ready to cheer for the next kicker and run to second, but there's a low rumble in the sky. Everyone stops what they're doing and looks up, including Marisol.

A second passes before the first raindrop falls.

"Rain," Marisol whispers to herself.

Another drop falls, then another.

Marisol imagines the clouds looking down on her.

Sorry we waited so long, but we wanted to give you time to kick the ball and run to at least one of the bases. Surely you understand.

Marisol nods.

"Yes," she says. "I understand."

GOOD

Dadhead calls that night, even though it's Thursday, because he wants to hear about Marisol's kickball game.

"Well, Scraps?" he says from the screen. "How was your big game?"

They're all sitting around the table—Marisol, Oz, and Mrs. Rainey. There are no nervous knots or angry seeds in Marisol's chest or belly. She feels like a butterfly. Light and happy.

"I kicked the ball and ran all the way to first base," Marisol says.

She waits for Oz to say something mean, like *First base? That's it?* or *First base is nothing—everyone gets to first base!* Instead, he bumps her shoulder, just like he does with his teammates on the Tornadoes.

"That's my sister—kickball queen!" he says.

Dadhead smiles. "I knew you could do it."

"I would've gone even farther if it hadn't

started raining," Marisol adds. "Maybe."

"No maybe about it," Dadhead says.

"Oz helped," Marisol adds.

Oz shrugs. "I just told her the ultimate rule— never take your eye off the ball."

"Good advice," Mrs. Rainey says.

Later, after they say goodbye to Dadhead and Marisol's hair is brushed and her tummy is full and it's time for bed, she gives Oz his soccer ball and tucks in all her stuffed animals. Then she crawls under her comforter. Beans stretches and curls into a ball at her feet.

Marisol lifts her head and looks at him. "Are you comfortable?" she asks.

Beans meows. Only once.

"Good," Marisol says.

And she closes her eyes, too.

Be on the lookout
for more
adventures with
Marisol!